THE BULLY BROTHERS

MAKING THE GRADE

by MIKE THALER · Illustrated by JARED LEE

SCHOLASTIC INC.
New York Toronto London Auckland Sydney

For Laurel Lee Thaler,
My Life, My Wife
— M.T.

To Andrea Brown,
Friend and Agent
— J.L.

ISBN 0-590-47801-X

Text copyright © 1995 by Mike Thaler.
Illustrations copyright © 1995 by Jared D. Lee Studio, Inc.
All rights reserved. Published by Scholastic Inc.

12 11 10 9 8 7 6 5 4 3 2 1   5 6 7 8 9/9 0/0

Printed in the U.S.A.   23

First Scholastic printing, September 1995

The Bully Brothers believed in getting good grades, so they always changed their report cards.

F's could easily be turned into A's with one line.
D's and C's were harder to change,
so they made sure they always got F's.

Their mom thought they were geniuses.

Their teacher knew they weren't.

So it was *very important*
to keep the two of them apart.

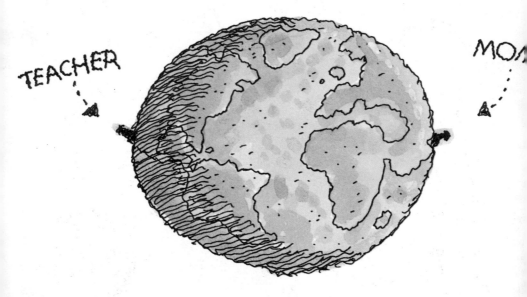

That's why when their teacher,
Miss Winky, announced PARENTS' NIGHT,
the Bully Brothers had a problem!

"We could send Mom to the wrong school,"
said Bubba.
"Bad idea," said Bumpo.

"We could dress like Miss Winky
and tell Mom how wonderful we are."
"Better," said Bumpo.

"I have it! We could dress like *Mom*,
and let Miss Winky tell us how stupid *we* are."
"Great idea!" smiled Bumpo.

So on PARENTS' NIGHT, Bubba and Bumpo told their mom it was canceled.

Then they quietly borrowed one of her dresses.
"I'll get on your shoulders," said Bubba,
"and we'll put on the dress."
"No way," said Bumpo. "I'll get on
your shoulders."

"Okay," said Bubba, "we'll flip."
"Okay," said Bumpo, calling *heads*
as the coin spun in the air.
But before it landed, he was already picturing
life on the bottom.

"It's tails," said Bubba, and he climbed up
on Bumpo's shoulders,
slipping the dress over both of them.
Then he put on a red wig, lipstick, and false eyelashes

"How do we look?" asked Bumpo.
"Great!" said Bubba, blinking his eyelashes
in the mirror.

It's a miracle how they got to school at all.
Bumpo bumped into every tree in the neighborhood,
with Bubba shouting,

"Look out!"

"Turn right!"

"Turn left!"

"Ouch!"

But they finally arrived,
and walked into Miss Winky's class.
"Good evening," said Bumpo
in his highest voice.

"And you must be . . ." said Miss Winky,
looking up.
"We're Bubba and Bumpo's mom,"
shrieked Bubba.

"Oh," said Miss Winky, blinking.
"I can see the resemblance."

"And how *are* my *little angels* doing?"

"Well, in all honesty, they're not doing well."

"Oh, goodness gracious," said Bubba,
blinking his eyelashes.
"And they work so hard at home."

"Well, they never hand in any *homework*."

"They're shy," said Bumpo,
from under the dress.
"What was that?" said Miss Winky.
"That's just my stomach grumbling," said Bubba,
whacking his stomach.
"Ouch," said Bumpo.
"Dinner's not sitting well," smiled Bubba.

"Well," said Miss Winky, "when they *do*
come to class, they're always late."
"It's because they take care of me
when I'm sick at home."
"What's wrong with you?" asked Miss Winky.
"An over-sensitive stomach," said Bubba.

"And this was their science project on animal camouflage!" said Miss Winky, holding up Stomper and Fang.

"Also, their behavior is not always
of the highest order."
"Boys will be boys," said Bubba, smiling.
"And I know how much they like you!"
"They do?" said Miss Winky.
"Oh, yes. They always talk about you."

"Not!" shouted Bumpo.
"Excuse me," said Bubba, poking his stomach.
"It's my disorder."
"Maybe I've misjudged the boys,"
said Miss Winky, deeply moved.

"Yes," said Bubba, blinking his eyelashes
as they walked toward the door.
"They're sweet, and kind, and—"
Just then, Bumpo bumped into the wall,
knocking Bubba off.

Miss Winky gasped at the mother,
who was now in two halves.

"It's nothing dear," said the Bubba half.
"Just part of my disorder."
And both halves ran out the door.

The next day, Miss Winky asked
if their mother felt better.
"She was beside herself when she got home,"
said Bubba.
"Stress!" said Bumpo.
"But she finally pulled herself together."
Bubba smiled.

After PARENTS' NIGHT, the boys' grades
went *down*.
Miss Winky, who was truly moved,
started tutoring them after school.

So their grades improved to D's,
which could only be turned into B's.
When their mom saw their grades drop, from
A's to B's, she started tutoring them at home, too.

"Don't worry boys," she said. "You'll get A's again."

"No matter how hard we try," sighed Bubba,
"it's impossible to be perfect."